CW00385015

WHISPER

SOPHIE CLOUD

Copyright © 2020 Sophie Cloud

All rights reserved.

ISBN: 979-8-6873-3769-4

DEDICATION

For Sam, Cindy, Patches, Juno and Echo

CONTENTS

ACKNOWLEDGEMENTS   vii

1   THE PUP   Page 1

2   OYSTER FISHING   Page 9

3   BAZ CALLUM   Page 18

4   WHISPER'S TRAINING   Page 26

5   THE CEASEFIRE   Page 32

6   HOMEWARD BOUND   Page 39

7   THE REUNION   Page 46

8   RETURN TO WAR   Page 62

9   NEW PLANS   Page 74

10   THREE SHELLS BEACH 1918-1919   Page 84

ACKNOWLEDGMENTS

Thanking the 50,000 canines who bravely carried messages and performed other duties in the field.

The old luxorious Romans vaunts did make
Of gustful oysters took in Lucrine Lake
Your Essex better hath and such perchance
As tempted Caeser first to pass through France

Sir Aston Cockain

'Whisper your name amid the noise of the howling sea then you will be saved. You lived and I named you Whisper.'

'Whisper your name on the fields of France and I will save you back.'

PROLOGUE

'Let me introduce myself. My name is Whisper. This is the story of my life. A life that isn't, or should I say wasn't an ordinary dog's life. Special they called me. I didn't see myself as special. I just completed the tasks that were set for me. I was just good at obeying. That way I would have my treats. I know I was clever in those days, and quite handsome for a terrier stray. I was found one cold winter morning by the salt marshes of Shoeburyness, near the sea, half hidden on a mound of sea-grass. It was December 1914, just before Christmas. I was cold and hungry and my heart was beating fast. I didn't know where my mother or father were and I was alone until a small pair of hands reached down, peeling back the grass and picking me up. A man-child had discovered me. His name was Ryan. How I loved him. This is the story of how Ryan saved me and how I saved others.'

CHAPTER 1 - THE PUP

DECEMBER 1914

Ryan had left school early that day. His plan was to smuggle the books back from the library. He would be able to make it in time if he went along the coastal road, onto Three Shells Beach and back towards the village. If he hurried, he would be back home before his stepfather had finished oyster fishing for the day. Not only was it Ryan's thirteenth birthday today, it was also a Wednesday. Maybe stepfather would be in the pub, he thought. The pub closed late on a Wednesday and maybe he wouldn't notice what time Ryan had arrived home. Taking off his shoes carefully so as not to get sand on them, he jumped from the pebbled road onto the damp softness beneath his cold toes. He knew he wasn't allowed on Three Shells Beach recently since his stepfather had forbidden him to go there for his constant 'backchat'.

Three Shells Beach was one of Ryan's favourite places in the world, second only to the library, so this was a punishment too far. Ryan would defy his stepfather today; after all it was his birthday. Humming to himself, he watched the Oystercatchers and the dark bellied Brent Geese swoop inland, and peck at whatever spoils they could find. When the oyster fisherman had left some of their catch behind, all number of birds would descend on Three Shells Beach but today there were no Grey Plovers, Bar-tailed Knots or Godwits or Redshanks. Stepfather had

taught him well on the comings and goings of the wild life
of the salt marshes but as he heard an unfamiliar cry
coming from a large bunch of sea-grass, he tried to drown
out the cries from the Dark Bellied geese to see what
creature was making this sound. Crouching down, Ryan
peeled back the thick strands of grass and there, lying in the
middle of it and cuddled up, cold and whimpering was a
new-born pup. Nervously he blew on his cold hands and
rubbed them together before carefully picking him up.
Light as a feather and still whimpering, Ryan held him up
to eye level, and looked deeply into the animals' warm
brown eyes. Cradling him to his chest and planting a soft
kiss on his black and white fury little head, Ryan pulled his
overcoat around him and looked about to see if there was
anybody else on the beach. There was no one. It was too
cold and windy and the Fishermen had now retired for the
day. Of course there was the coastguard's cottage just
above him along the jetty. He knew Jack Leemer lived
there. His mother had mentioned him, and Ryan had seen
him only a few weeks ago collecting oysters in the marshes.
He had waved at Ryan, but Ryan had ignored him. He was
old and strange, with a long white beard and he talked to
himself. Looking about him again, he realised his only
option was to see if Jack Leemer was at home. Ryan could
tell the pup was barely alive as his whimpering had
quietened now, and his breathing seemed shallow. Ryan
was too frightened to check. He scrambled up the pebbled
bank and onto the jetty. A white flag attached to a tall black
mast on the porch of the pebble-dashed cottage waved

furiously in the wind. Grey shutters on the ground floor windows banged viciously, making Ryan jump just as he was about to knock on the weather-beaten door. He stepped back and had second thoughts about asking this man for help. Maybe he could leave the pup just there. Surely the man would find it eventually, he thought. Rubbing his forehead he looked about him for something to place the pup in. There were a few plant pots a couple of feet away. Ryan placed the sleeping pup gently down onto the ground so as not to disturb it. He then set to dragging the heavy pot nearer to the door, ready to place the dog in it. Just then he felt a rough and heavy hand on his shoulder, and a bellowing voice in his ear.

'What do you think you are doing, you lout?' screamed the old man in Ryan's ear.

Ryan felt his shoulder's stiffen, a familiar feeling and his heart began to beat fast - an uncomfortable rhythm he knew so well. Ryan turned around and saw it was Jack Leemer, his beard shaking under the wobbly chin, his eyes ablaze with anger.

'Nothing. I wanted to ask for your help. I'm Ryan Kelly,' said Ryan in a whispery voice.

The old man let go of his grip, and reached in his pocket for his glasses. Putting them on and squinting at Ryan he said 'Aye, I can see now, your Mary's son, Don Kelly's boy.' Ryan nodded. 'So why are you moving my pot?'

'I was going to put the Pup I found in it. I… didn't know

what to do with him,' Ryan said, sheepishly.

'Pup, did you say?' Jack asked.

Ryan nodded, pointing to his coat by the front door. 'He's in there,' he said.

'I hope this isn't some joke. I've had enough pranksters around here lately,' said the old man bending down slowly to peer inside the coat. 'Aye, it's a young terrier, and barely alive by the looks of it.'

Picking him up with one large hand and opening the front door with the other, he gestured to Ryan with a nod of his head for Ryan to follow him indoors. Ryan hesitated.

'Come on, I don't bite. Besides I need you to help me save this young'un. Just a whisper of a heartbeat left I fear,' Jack explained.

Quickly Ryan followed Jack into the cottage. Small but cosy, with a fire left burning, it smelt of wood smoke. The one thing that struck Ryan the most was that the room was entirely covered in wall-to-wall bookshelves, filled with many colours of books of all sizes.

'Quick, don't dawdle, you'll let the heat out,' Jack said gruffly. 'Shut the door and follow me into the kitchen,' he instructed, noticing the boy gawping at his books.

Jack was already searching through draws and rummaging loudly as Ryan sauntered into the kitchen.

'I need one of those eye droppers, you know the glass ones,' said Jack passing the bundle to Ryan. 'Ah, got it, knew it would be here,' he said, relieved.

Collecting some paraphernalia from the fridge he instructed Ryan to place the pup on the newly sanded kitchen table. Out came eggs, vegetable oil and some condensed milk. Grabbing a bowl he broke the eggs into it, pouring in the condensed milk and oil.

'Pass me the dropper will you please?' the old man instructed. Pouring the mixture through a funnel into the dropper, Jack carefully placed the rubber teat back on. 'This should do the trick if the little'un will take it,' said Jack. 'Life or death, which do you choose little'un?'

Taking the pup out from the blanket, Jack rubbed its head and stroked its nose as if to awaken it. Squeezing the teat until a drop of liquid oozed out, Jack stuck it under the pup's nose. For a second he didn't respond, and then with a little lift of the head and a twitch of the nose, he turned in the direction of the teat. Jack pushed the teat into its mouth and the pup began to suckle.

'There,' said Jack to Ryan, in a whisper. 'I think this little chap chooses life. So what shall we name him?'

Excitedly Ryan earnestly locked eyes with the old man. 'Whisper of course,' he said knowingly as if it couldn't be anything else.

'Perfect,' acknowledged Jack, enjoying the puppy's new

enthusiasm for life with Ryan. 'There, that will bring him back to life. Just a few more drops and then we can let him go back to sleep,' said the old man stroking Whisper's small head.

Ryan watched intently. Jack was obviously experienced at this. 'How did you know what to do?' asked Ryan, impressed at the gentleness of this gruff old coastguard.

'Brought up on a farm, but that wasn't the life for me. The sea had my calling!' Jack exclaimed.

Ryan nodded. He knew what he wanted to be when he was older, but no one in his family would listen. They heard but pretended they didn't. Ryan followed Jack into the sitting room and watched him take a blanket from the back of the armchair to make a little bed near the fire and place the sleeping Whisper down into it.

'Would you like a cup of tea?' asked Jack again noticing Ryan's curiosity in his vast book collection.

'Yes please,' answered Ryan self-consciously.

'Good, then after you can take the pup home.'

'I can't,' said Ryan firmly. Jack raised an eyebrow.

'You don't want to keep Whisper?' asked Jack stoking the fire and pushing Whisper a little further away from the heat.

'It's not that. I would love to keep him, but my stepfather

would never let me.'

'I see,' said Jack getting up slowly and walking back into the kitchen.

Ryan sat nervously on the old chintz covered chair, knowing he would be late home if he stayed any longer. As Jack brought the tea out to Ryan, the boy jumped up.

'Think I'd better be going.' he said, not meeting the old man's eyes. Jack eyed the boy sympathetically.

'Well if you want I can keep Whisper for a few days and then we can think what to do with him?' Jack asked.

Ryan nodded, feeling relieved. Jack opened the front door and Ryan shyly thanked him, and then quickly, without turning around ran back down towards the beach and on towards home. Jack shook his head, closed the front door and sat next to Whisper by the fire. Sipping on his tea he wondered what had startled the boy and why he was in such a hurry. Later he noticed Ryan had left his coat on the kitchen table.

'Don't you worry Whisper he'll be back to see you tomorrow.' Jack muttered, cradling the dog on his lap.

That night, Jack couldn't sleep. Eventually he brought Whisper up to his bedroom to keep an eye on him. There was no point, he thought, worrying about Whisper being downstairs alone, and him lying awake upstairs. Making himself a hot chocolate, adding a splash of rum to help him sleep and after feeding Whisper again, Jack chose himself a book, crooked Whisper under one arm, his drink and book under the other, and walked slowly upstairs. He turned on his bedroom lamp and placing the pup on an old newspaper at the bottom of his bed, got back under the patchwork quilt. Sitting upright with the pillows plumped behind him and began to read, occasionally sipping his hot drink whilst he eyed Whisper sleeping soundly. The wind was howling outside but the pup was silently happy, curled up and full of milk. After an hour Whisper stirred and Jack cradled him in his arms and laid a kiss on his head.

'How I'd love to keep you my friend but I can't. I'm too old to take you for the walks you will need,' he said under his breath.

Jack however, had another idea for Whisper. Placing the pup back to the bottom of the bed, he at last felt at peace knowing this decision was the right one for Whisper.

CHAPTER 2 – OYSTER FISHING

'No sea, swale or harbinger can destroy it if you take care of your oyster catcher'

'Where's he going now?' Don Kelly shouted at his wife and stepson, feeling exasperated as he felt his authority being continually undermined as they stood by the front door whispering.

'Don, leave him alone, he needs to go to the library and collect some books for school,' Mary said, nervously standing up for her son.

Don Kelly rose from the breakfast table. His manner threatening, but he was too tired for a fight this morning. He had been up all night worrying about money.

'Quick, go, but don't be late back tonight,' Ryan's mother said, kissing him on his cheek.

Mary knew her husband's moods. She could tell he didn't want to argue this morning but she had to tread carefully.

'You baby that boy Mary!' he said, now throwing his plate into the kitchen sink.

'I do no such thing. He's only thirteen,' she said quietly, going to the sink to wash up the breakfast plates.

'He may be thirteen but I have an eye out for him. I know he goes to the beach when he should be home. I see him, you don't. He can come fishing with me tomorrow. Take the day off school!' he demanded.

Mary wanted to argue back, but she thought better of it. She could see her husband was tired and worried. Grabbing his coat and tinderbox and placing his cap upon his head, he turned back to his wife as he opened the front door.

'He can get all those thoughts of being a teacher out of his befogged brain. We need money coming into this house, not money going out for school and college. And you know there are lads making a wage as soldiers out in France,' he continued.

'And you know where that leads, Don Kelly,' said Mary looking squarely into her husband's eyes. He is thirteen, not sixteen!' Mary shuddered when he finally walked out after slamming the door shut. Ringing her hands together she said under her breath 'Lets hope this war doesn't continue.'

Ryan was running now. He knew his stepfather would not be far behind. He had to make it to Three Shells Beach for a quick detour to see Whisper and get to the library on time. His heart was pounding. Thoughts were racing through his head. 'What if Whisper wasn't there?' he thought. 'Fifteen minutes until opening time, twelve minutes to see Whisper,' Ryan repeated to himself as he ran, occasionally turning around to see if he was being followed. He could feel beads of sweat roll down his brow as he rapped on Jack Leemer's door. Ryan was counting every second. One minute, two, then the door opened.

'I've come to see Whisper,' said Ryan clearing his throat to cover his nervousness.

'Aye, so you have,' Jack answered looking relaxed and jovial in a navy blue sweater that could keep out the coldest of weathers. 'He's by the fire. Sit down and make yourself at home.'

Ryan marched in almost as if he was possessively claiming his pup. His heart melted as he clapped eyes on the snuffling black and white puppy moving about on the blanket.

'He's a strong one, that one… would you like a cup of tea?' asked Jack, peering round the door, holding the kettle.

'No thanks. I have to get to the library before school. I have to go soon,' responded Ryan.

Jack put the kettle down, amused at the young man who would walk through his front door and as quick as a flash would announce that he would be leaving! Smiling, he put his head around the door again to see the young man holding the puppy tightly, lifting him up, and letting Whisper lick his cheeks.

'Library you say? Well, I have a library here. You can choose a book if you like and borrow it,' he said, pointing to the bookshelf on the left.

Ryan's eyes lit up. If he borrowed a book from Jack he could stay with Whisper another five and a half minutes. 'What did you say?' asked Jack hearing the boy mumble to himself.

'I said yes please.'

'Good, then sit down. You are making me nervous,' Jack remarked, shaking his head at this young man.

Pouring the tea carefully, he passed a bone china cup to Ryan who tentatively took it. Then he walked across the room to pick a few books that Ryan may like. 'How about this one? The Adventures of Tom Sawyer by Mark Twain. Have you read it?' he asked.

Ryan shook his head. Jack passed the book over to him, and then looked out for another. 'Have you read Jules Verne, Twenty Thousand Leagues Under the Sea?' as he stretched for the large book.

Again, Ryan shook his head. 'Good', said Jack, 'that will keep you busy until next week. Can you manage to finish them?'

'I'll try', said Ryan putting Whisper down on his lap as Jack passed the books to him.

Tipping his head back to finish the last drop of his tea, Ryan got up to leave, putting Whisper back into his basket. Ryan turned to the old man. 'Thank you for looking after him.'

Taking some shillings out of his coat pocket, he held out his hand for Jack to take them.

'What's that for?' the old man said rather surprised.

'For looking after Whisper and for buying him the basket,' he retorted shyly.

'Don't be so daft, but don't think you are going to get away lightly. You'll have to train him with me. I have an idea for him,' said Jack, looking smug.

Ryan placed his pocket money back into his coat, tipped his cap at Jack and ran out of the door. As he ran alongside the sand dunes, he knew he was going to be late. Checking his watch again, he knew it would take one minute and at least forty-five seconds to get to school. Ryan timed everything he did. It was essential for him. It kept him safe and out of trouble. He could see the red brick school building in the distance and with forty-five seconds to go; he counted backwards as a red kite swooped overhead. It's high-pitched mewing ringing in Ryan's ears. Entering Collins Road, the kite hovered above him, its widespread wings looming hauntingly in the wind as if waiting for Ryan to enter the school gates. Its yellow eyes watching Ryan until he disappeared inside. The bird of prey then disappeared out of sight. Ryan thought maybe he had imagined it. They were pretty rare around here and only once had Ryan seen one before when he was in his stepfather's boat. Mr Rawlings, the Headmaster, was standing at the gates this morning. Ryan tried to keep his head down. He didn't want the Headmaster seeing him late again. But the Headmaster was more interested in the kite that had been hovering overhead.

'Did you see that Ryan?'

'Yes Sir.' Ryan replied, trying not to catch his eye.

'It is Ryan Kelly, isn't it?'

'Yes Sir.'

'Hurry up in then, and oh before I forget, your Father dropped off your pencil case this morning, and said you would be taking the day off tomorrow for an eye test.'

Ryan raised his eyebrows. He knew he had placed his pencil case in his school bag last night. Ryan's face paled. That man was always nosing about his business.

'Everything all right at home Ryan? You look worried,' said the Headmaster, suddenly distracted by another pupil who was running through the gates.

'No sir, everything's fine thank you,' replied Ryan again avoiding Mr Rawling's eye.

'Good, good, glad you are keeping up the hard work.'

'Yes Sir,' said Ryan passing Mr Rawlings and making his way to his classroom.

*

The kite was back and it wasn't long before it was encircling the boat. 'Haven't seen one of those around for a long time,' said Ryan's stepfather, as he hauled a fishing basket into the back of the pretty blue boat.

It was a cold morning, and this was the last thing Ryan wanted to be doing. It was the last few days before term ended and it was the last day of rehearsals of the school play. Why his stepfather had wanted him to fish with him today, he didn't know. He could only he could imagine he knew Ryan was up to something and he was determined to get it out of him. Don Kelly always made it his business to know what everyone was up to in the family. His elder brother Josh had now left home and had joined a steel works in Liverpool. At twenty years old, Josh was too big to be pushed around by the likes of Don Kelly. His sister Vivien had a little more freedom, but at sixteen she still wasn't allowed to have a boyfriend. She kept herself to herself mostly, working part-time in the local post office. But it was Ryan that he bothered. Watching him like a hawk.

'Pull the nets in Ryan,' his stepfather barked at him. As the oyster net was pulled in, Don Kelly ordered Ryan to check the size of the oysters. 'Too small and you will have to put it back. We don't want no spats.' he instructed.

Ryan took out an oyster that he was unsure of and placed it in the size checker - a small metal loop that the oyster could slip through easily if they were too small. It would be tossed back to grow to have its freedom, whatever its fate on that day. Only a certain amount of oysters could be caught and this was a good way of keeping down the numbers. After an hour of repeating the same process Don Kelly maneuvered the boat back to shore. As they neared their mooring, Ryan caught sight of Jack Leemer staring out to sea from the jetty. He recognised Ryan and waved. Ryan was too afraid to wave back.

'Who's that silly old coot waving to?' snarled Don Kelly now tired from his morning fishing.

Ryan just shrugged, hoping Jack wouldn't meet them on the shore. As Ryan looped the rope around the mooring, he could see Jack had met someone else on the beach and was far too deep in conversation to notice them pulling in their catch of the day and heaving it over to the shed near the larger boats.

'You enjoyed today then son?' asked Don Kelly triumphant at their plentiful catch.

'Yes sir,' said Ryan nervously.

'To think I may make a fisherman out of you yet,' he said patting the boy on the back. Ryan stiffened, not used to such friendly banter with his stepfather.

His mother had the tea on the table when they got back. Ryan went to wash his hands. 'Twenty shillings we made mother. Aye, what do you think about that?' said Don hanging up his hat and coat.

'Well done my lads,' said Mrs Kelly trying to keep the peace. She knew how changeable Don Kelly's moods were these days, so she agreed with everything he said. She wasn't sure when she had started agreeing with everything he said, but she knew she had changed too. Once the fiery women who knew her own mind, now she had become timid and she didn't like herself for it. Once Ryan is old enough to leave home, things would change. She would change, she told herself.

CHAPTER 3 – BAZ CALLUM

SEPTEMBER 1915

The kite was flying high before the red dawn, surfing the sea for a mollusc or two. Guzzling an oyster for its prey, it soared from the marshes in land and hovered over the barracks. One soldier contemplating his fate, a young man of twenty-one called Baz Callum, out guarding the barracks, watched as the red kite settled on a crossroads. It's wings outstretched, watching Baz and he watched it too. In it's beak, an oyster shell which he dropped dutifully at Baz's feet and flew off. Baz stubbed out his cigarette and yawned. 'Where was his relief Sergeant,' he wondered? He had to ask the Sergeant's permission to leave Coggeshall and go to Shoeburyness[1] to the dog-training centre. Growing up in Canada outside Ottowa on a farm, he raised six dogs of his own. He was keen to volunteer to work with dogs wherever this may lead. Used to an adventure, the tall dark Canadian had followed his mother over to England last year where she married four years ago. He had been in the Essex regiment for six months. As soon as the war was imminent, he knew he wanted to enlist as soon as possible. His chance of using his skills with the dogs that he so loved meant he knew where his immediate future lay. Baz was still getting used to the British way of life. It wasn't easy but

---

[1] In 1917, Lieutenant Colonel Richardson founded the British War Dog School in Shoeburyness, Essex to train Messenger Dogs.

he enjoyed the camaraderie of the men. The days seemed to emerge into one long role of training, fitness and planning, in anticipation for the call for his battalion to be called up for war in France.

'You think it could be something you would be good at then?' asked Sergeant Privers, ticking and signing Baz's pass for the day to travel to the dog-training centre in Shoeburyness.

'As I said sir, I have trained six dogs of my own. All working dogs, sheepdogs on the farm in Canada,' said Baz, now saluting his officer and taking the pass from him.

'Very good then. Perhaps when you get a better idea of the situation you could recruit a few other men too. See what it's all about then, Private Callum,' said Sergeant Privers happy to wave this young man off for the day.

Baz caught the 10.05am train to Shoeburyness. It was a bittersweet day and as he sat in the carriage he wasted no time in opening a map and pinpointing where he was heading for the dog-training centre. Momentarily distracted by the sneezing of a fellow soldier opposite him, he looked out through the windows to the marshlands not far from Shoeburyness itself. Droplets of rain raced each other down the misty windowpanes and Baz could see the beginnings of a rainbow. How the sun had shone an hour ago as he had walked to the station, warm enough for him to adjust his stiff military collar and clear his throat uncomfortably. He hadn't had the time for a cup of tea at the station as the train had pulled in earlier than expected. He would find a tea place as soon as he arrived. Wishing he had brought his umbrella, Baz ran from the train to the nearest teahouse next to the station, marching through the door and settling himself down in a booth. The teahouse was full of soldiers from the Essex Battalion out with their girlfriends. A pretty blond girl sat quietly with her soldier love in the far side of the café as the waitress served them. She was giggling with the young man in the khaki uniform and whispering something in his ear. Baz looked away for a moment, embarrassed he had caught himself staring. He turned to the view of the sea, and by the fence which was bordering it, where the rushes grew high, he saw a bird perched on the white wooden post. It was a red kite. Baz recognised the bird of prey, similar to the ones where he grew up by the lake in Ottowa. Although seen regularly here as the oysters were equally plentiful, it seemed too much of a coincidence to see another in such a short space of time. As Baz waited patiently to be served, the kite sat calmly. Baz could make out his large eyes almost staring directly at him. He knew them to be yellow although he couldn't see them from this far away. It wasn't until the waitress finally came to serve Baz, taking a menu, he let his interest on the bird waver. When he returned his gaze, he saw it was getting ready to fly off. Its speed as it took off made the bird look almost ethereal in the mist. Its wings eerily fully outstretched. As it soared and spiraled skyward the waitress cleared her throat impatiently.

'May I have a pot of tea please?' Baz asked the young

waitress as she impatiently tapped her pen on her notebook. 'And may I ask, Ma'am, if you know where the War Dog School is?'

The waitress stared at the soldier intently for a second or two as if she recognised him but couldn't place where she had seen him before. She then turned around, and motioned towards another soldier.

'See that soldier there with his girlfriend? That's Sam. I think he works there,' explained the waitress. She then beckoned to the young soldier who had looked up from his conversation with the blond. He got up and sauntered over to Baz.

'Can I help you?' he asked. Baz noticed the girlfriend eyeing the waitress jealously.

'Sam, this gentleman wants directions to the War Dog School. Can you help him?' asked the waitress.

'Baz Callum, pleased to meet you!' he said to his fellow soldier.

'You American?' Sam asked with a quizzical look.

'No, Canadian, but I live at the Coggeshall Barracks,' he answered, used to people thinking he was Amcrican.

'Are you training a dog at the school?' Sam asked, wondering if he had left his dog outside.

'Well no, I'm just doing some enquiries for my Sergeant. I

would like to and some of my fellow soldiers from my battalion want to as well.'

'Do you have a dog in mind?' asked Sam, now turning to smile at his girlfriend who was tapping at her watch impatiently.

'Not yet. Just thought I would take some notes today, meet people and get an idea of how many dogs we could train with the school,' explained Baz feeling he was rather in at the deep end with all this now.

'No worries. I can take you up there now if you like. I am a handler myself. I have my own dog, a terrier. She's outside,' Sam said, pointing out to below the windowsill to where Betty, his dog, was tied.

'Terriers are good,' Sam continued, signaling to his girlfriend to leave.

'How far is the school from here? Walking distance?' asked Baz, now noticing the dark clouds forming over the café. The rain was coming down in torrents.

'I have my lorry outside. I can take you. You don't want to be walking in this weather,' replied the helpful soldier.

'Sam I thought we were going to the pictures?' whined the pretty girlfriend as she rolled her eyes and reached for her raincoat.

'We can get the later showing Irene. We must give this chap a lift. He has come all the way from Coggeshall.'

'Look,' stated Baz, 'I don't want to put you two out, really I don't,' Baz said realising his presence was causing a problem between the couple.

'Oh don't take any notice of Irene,' said Sam pulling the pretty girl onto his knee and planting a kiss on her forehead.

'Listen Irene, go and do some shopping and I will meet you in an hour. We can get back for the 3 o'clock showing!' Sam said now turning back to Baz. Chewing some gum, Irene just shrugged and walked out of the café.

'I hope I haven't caused a fight between you,' Baz said to Sam putting on his coat and feeling rather sheepish.

'No, she will be fine,' said Sam, leaving a tip for the waitress. 'I will meet her later, and if I'm honest I could do with some male company. She always wants to be with me when I'm on leave, though I don't blame her. She worries for me. She is all I have in this world apart from my other love of my life outside!'

'Who?' asked Baz confused for a moment.

'Betty of course! My little black terrier outside!' cried Sam, thinking this Baz chap was amusing. He smiled to himself as he grabbed his keys.

*

That afternoon, Baz watched an old man and a boy of about thirteen or fourteen put their young terrier through its paces. The old bearded man stood at the sidelines whilst the boy ran alongside the dog willing it to run faster - as fast as the other dogs training in his group.

'Come on Whisper! This way, that way!' shouted the boy. Baz could see this boy and this dog had a strong connection. The young terrier eyed his master almost with adoration.

'Be more masterful!' shouted the old man from the sidelines, although Baz was doubtful the boy and his dog could hear him.

Whisper looked to Baz as if he was having the time of his life. All the other dogs had masters in their uniforms. He wondered why this boy and the old man were allowed out here on the field.

'Is that usual?' Baz asked Sam as he pointed to the boy and his dog.

'Sometimes,' explained Sam, 'When the dogs are first being recruited, they come in with their existing owners,' said Sam now looking at his watch and wanting to make his goodbyes to his new friend.

'It's kind of sad don't you think?' said Baz, realising that the dog and his young master would be parted one day, maybe soon.

'That's life I suppose. Life of a messenger dog,' said Sam matter-of-factly.

Baz couldn't keep his eyes off the young dog and as the sun peeped through the clouds, the kite appeared again, not taking his beady eyes off the young dog. It circled the field a few times, its glorious wings at full span, it's golden eyes twinkling in the sun. Then suddenly as fast as it had appeared, it flew off in the direction of the sea. Baz sighed. He would have to approach the pair and ask them whether he could perhaps take on the role as Soldier Master for their messenger dog. And this he did.

CHAPTER 4 – WHISPER'S TRAINING

It's not the size of the dog in the fight, it's the size of the fight in the dog. – Mark Twain

'I think he would be ready for training now,' said Jack, pleased that Ryan had at last taken his nose out of his latest book.

Sighing with delight at the exciting ending of his novel, Ryan stretched out his arms above his head, yawning and then turning his attention to Whisper. The terrier lay at his feet waiting to be fed by his master. He was already licking his salty paws from the marshes looking hungry. Snow was beginning to settle around the decking of the coastguard's cottage, and Ryan, pleased that the sea was too rough to have fished for oysters that morning with his stepfather, instead enjoyed the peace and quiet of Jack's cottage and spending time with Whisper. Jack brought in a steaming pot of tea and some lemon cake and placed it down on a nestle table next to the fire.

'Take Whisper out quickly before the snow settles. The tea will keep for a few minutes,' instructed Jack, now pulling the heavy curtains closed to keep in the warmth of the room. Ryan did as he was instructed. He put on his overcoat and called to Whisper who had yet to get up from lying by the fire. 'I think it's time that dog starts his official training before he gets too lazy,' said Jack with a wink to Ryan, thinking that Whisper needed a good walk and a better regime. 'That nice soldier would be a perfect Soldier Master for him,' said Jack knowing Ryan would agree with him. Whisper put his nose in the snow. It was cold and he lapped up the droplets on his face.

'Come on boy!' instructed Ryan as he marched towards the sea for a brisk walk. Along the dunes they walked and just as Ryan was about to turn around to go back to the cottage he could see his sister running towards him far in the distance, her slender arms flaring around her trying to get his attention. Ryan stopped. What was it now, he thought. Mother and his stepfather had been arguing furiously of late as Don Kelly had been stuck at home, and not out fishing in the mornings. The sea had been too rough. His stepfather's frustration had been plain to see by everybody in the family. His sister Vivien's new boyfriend had already intervened in an argument between his mother and his stepfather yesterday with Don swinging punches at the poor bloke. Vivien had been left in tears as the poor boyfriend swore never to come back to the house ever again.

'You have to come back quickly, and leave that dog alone for goodness sake,' she said out of breath. 'Your mother has been taken sick this afternoon, and the doctor is with her now. He says it maybe her heart.'

Tears pricked Ryan's eyes. He nodded at his sister, feeling the shock enveloping him, and said that he would follow once he had taken Whisper back to Jack's house. Running along the beach with Whisper at his heels, and feeling the wind bite at his face, he encouraged Whisper to run at the same pace. Whisper's ears pulled back as he eyed his master as they ran towards the sandy porch of Jack Leemer's house. Ryan patted Whisper's head to say goodbye as he left the dog by Jack's feet.

'Mind you stop by on Monday and we will take Whisper to the dog training school. Ten o' clock sharp!' Jack called to the harried lad as Ryan spun on his heels. The old man added, 'I hope your mother is all right.'

Ryan heard him clearly as the wind carried the old man's voice along the shore. The ferns bristled as Ryan ran through them, the sea salt hitting him in the face. He shielded his eyes as he counted his steps back home. The kite swooped low, mewing over Ryan's head. His wings were at full span now, hovering protectively over the boy. Ryan had got used to the frequent sightings of the kite, and it was almost normal for him to feel him around as he came and went about his business. It didn't occur to him that whenever something of note was happening to him the kite seemed to appear.

His mother was in bed and his sister was in the kitchen talking to Doctor Partridge. The doctor was explaining some symptoms to Vivien and thought perhaps his mother had tuberculosis.

'I will not know for sure until we take her to hospital in

London for further tests. I'll make enquiries this afternoon and come back later this afternoon once I have made arrangements for an ambulance. We cannot take unnecessary risks to her life and yours and Ryan's,' he explained, noticing Ryan listening by the door. 'Now do we know where she may have caught this?' he asked the pair of them, taking a notebook out of his brief case.

'Gosh, I have no idea but there was the baby at Yew Tree Cottage that had a bout of influenza recently but to my mind I can't think of where else she has been,' said Vivien puzzled and nervous for her mother.

'What about those stowaways that came in on that rowing boat stepfather talked about last week,' ventured in Ryan.

'I thought that was just hearsay. Someone said a dead soldier was found on the beach but I thought that was just fishermen's talk,' replied Vivien wringing her hands nervously.

'I will make enquiries about that,' said Doctor Partridge. 'When was that exactly?' he asked, looking to Vivien.

'I would say about a month ago,' she replied looking to Ryan. 'Wasn't it Ryan? The coastguard, Mr Leemer, had alerted the police guard, did he not?'

'Yes', replied Ryan. 'Jack caught them skulking around the coastguard cottage early one morning. There was some talk that they were German.'

'You spend too much time with Mr Leemer, Ryan,' said his

sister now feeling agitated with the situation and irritable with Ryan.

'Well there's no need to worry about that right now. The main thing is to get your mother looked after. Where is Mr Kelly?' Doctor Partridge enquired, looking to the pair of them.

'Probably fishing,' said Ryan. His sister sighed. She knew where her stepfather was but she wasn't about to tell Ryan or the doctor. His sister fetched her coat from the stand and said 'Ryan I'm going to fetch stepfather. You wait here until I get back. Don't leave mother!' Ryan was annoyed by his sister's assumption that he would ever leave his mother while she needed him. He wasn't Don Kelly. He sat down by the kitchen fire as his sister hurried to the front door. She turned around before she opened it, looking tired and her face pinched with worry. 'Why', he thought, 'do we all have to run around after that man? If he isn't here now why does it matter? Don Kelly really doesn't care about anyone else.' Ryan hated him now. His mother deserved better.

'Vivien, I will walk out with you', said Doctor Partridge, closing his briefcase and putting on his hat. 'Will you be going to the tavern at the corner of Boot Street?'

'No, not this time. I'm going towards the village. I know where he is though,' she said, pursing her lips. Her hand reached the top button of her coat, and struggling to fasten it, she stopped and pulled the latch on the door. The young doctor looked perplexed and Ryan could tell he wanted to discuss things with Vivien without Ryan being present.

'Goodnight Ryan. I will call back later on my evening rounds. If she takes a turn for the worse, you know where I live sonny!' he said, soothingly. Vivien walked out through the door with the doctor, shutting it behind them.

'What is the prognosis, Doctor? I don't want Ryan to worry,' Vivien asked.

Tipping his hat at Vivien, he cleared his throat. 'Only time will tell I'm afraid, Vivien', he stated. 'Let's get her needs met first.'

Ryan turned back to the fire. His face feeling the heat, but the rest of him was cold. Why wasn't it Don Kelly that was ill, not mother, he thought, bitterly. Stoking the fire and then kicking a cinder that had fallen out of the hearth, he was alerted to a cry from upstairs. He pushed his hair out of his eyes and followed the sound of distress upstairs.

CHAPTER 5 – THE CEASEFIRE

JUNE 1916

'For God's sake hold on, we will relieve you tomorrow'

Baz, Whisper and the other men were approaching Fort Douaumont, Verdun in an attempt to capture it. On the first night Whisper was nervous. He knew his training. He zigzagged along the sharp and stony earth. Keep going. Do not hesitate. Drown out the sound of mortar bombs and shouts. Keep going, even when the kite screeches at you from above, as it warns you the dangers ahead. This could be your time. Beware with every fibre of your being, he thought to himself. He knew he was going to have to run fast, and that night he dreamt he was back amongst the fens, along Three Shells Beach with Ryan and Jack Leemer. He sighed a contented sigh. Homeward bound. He would be home soon, wouldn't he? He licked his lips and put his soft snout down upon the pads of his paws. It was all right to be nervous. He knew the kite would watch out for him from above. He was going to do the very best for his master. He knew his mission. He knew that the brass tube attached to his back was there for a purpose. The carrier pigeons, which were sometimes attached to his harness when needed, were ready to go too.

The second Essex battalion marched forth to the Fort. Baz

was quiet. He always went quiet when he was nervous. The fort had already been bombed. Plenty of rubble now lay at their feet. Whisper's paws suddenly felt sore and a dusty yellow hue enveloped his black paws with grit seeping in between his now hardening pads. He winced. He looked up to his soldier master for reassurance. He could see his master was weary. His eyes sunken and his back arching as he stretched. His uniform restricted his movements. He loosened his collar. The starchy, itchy collar which he hated. He had heard his master recite the words *Whisper my name on the field of France and I will rescue you back*. He knew when Baz told him this today it would be his time to run. Run for his life, and save the lives of the second Essex battalion if he could. Save us Whisper! You can do it, he thought he heard them say, and he knew he could. He imagined Ryan saying this to him.

He remembered being put in a fishing basket as Don Kelly and Ryan set out to sea to catch oysters a few months back. The red kite swooped overhead having already flown back from France that day. 'Will that damn bird ever go away?' Whisper remembered Don Kelly say under his breath as he let loose the empty baskets into the sea to catch the oysters. The kite settled down on the side of the blue fishing boat, watching for the oysters that were being trapped in the baskets, one eye on Don Kelly and one eye on Whisper. Ryan had hoped his stepfather wouldn't notice the little pup in the spare basket nestled between their lunch and his stepfather's large black boots. 'Quiet Whisper', said the young boy with his fingers on his lips, and quiet Whisper was as the gentle rocking of the boat sent him into a slumber.

Baz put the message into the brass tube. Today he hadn't attached the carrier pigeon to Whispers' back. He had the message now and he knew he had to relay it and do his job well. Setting off to the enemy lines, Whisper's mission had begun. Whisper crouched down. He saw the barbed wire and crawled underneath it. He saw men in different uniforms to the ones he was used to. A different hue to the ones he had grown familiar with. He approached the men stealthily. A German soldier caught hold of his collar and pulled Whisper to him. The soldier beckoned his fellow comrades to approach the dog. The soldier spoke to him in a language he hadn't heard before. A cry went up and then nothing. The soldier put his hands on his lips as if to show Whisper he could not bark at that moment. He was then picked up by the scruff of the neck by another larger man, known for his rough treatment towards the other soldiers and taken into their dugout.

It was the battle of Verdun. Baz and the Essex battalion were approaching a dugout in Fort Douaumont. Surrounding the fort was a moat but it had dried out due to the heat. The tunnel had been left undefended and the Germans had conquered it for the time being. Taking the collar from around the dog's neck and retrieving the message, three German soldiers sat at a table with Whisper in between them deciding what to do next. Raised voices could be heard. '*Klingt gut*' said one soldier, giving the others a nod. Looking to Whisper the superior officer shrugged his shoulders and ordered 'We will have a ceasefire for two hours. Return this dog and give us all some time.'

Baz and the Essex battalion were walking slowly now, hearing shells overhead and gradually stalking the ground nearer to the entrance of the tunnel of Fort Douaumont. There were thirty-nine of them in all, mainly younger men with only a few over forty years of age. Two of them were still holding onto their own messenger dogs. Their sergeant, David Moore, walked ahead alone with his bayonet tucked awkwardly at his side. Baz caught up with him and untwisted his bayonet belt. He could tell his sergeant was as nervous as himself, and Baz was worried for Whisper too.

'How far do we go without us regrouping?' Baz asked, almost wanting to delay time and change tactics. He felt they were undermanned and sitting ducks as a light began to shine on them from the Fort.

'Stop!' ordered Sergeant Moore. 'Get down!' he screamed.

The men began to relay the command behind them. 'Get down! Get down!' The dogs crouched and the men lay in the rubble. Their hearts beating fast, not knowing if they were going to get out of this situation alive.

'*Lass den Hund laufen*!' shouted the German soldier to Whisper, clapping his hands together to try to get the dog to run away. Whisper's ears pricked up. A message had been put back into his collar and now the German soldier had patted him hard on his hind legs and he was being sent on his way. Torchlight could be seen in the distance and he started to follow it. He picked up speed but he heard a mewing from above. It was the kite circling him. Which way, he thought to himself.. Should he follow the torchlight or follow the bird of prey soaring above him? He slowed down, confused. He crouched for a moment, his tail lowering with nervousness. 'What would Ryan have done?' All those times along Three Shells Beach and all those minutes they counted to run back to Jack Leemer's cottage avoiding Don Kelly returning from his afternoon's drinking. 'We followed the Kite then, didn't we? Didn't we make it? Didn't we stay out of trouble then?' he thought, his tail starting to rise. He got up and shook himself, making a slight slapping sound as the message tin rattled quietly around his neck. He decided to ignore the light and follow the kite. Orders had gone up for Baz and the men to change tactics and move to the left. The searchlights were above them and they had to move nearer to the trees for cover. Meanwhile, Whisper was shivering slightly out of nervousness but then calmed down when the British soldier gave him some water. He had made it back to the Essex battalion.

'Good boy,' said Corporal Maxwell Peters as he looked around for Baz. 'There Whisper, there's your master. Go!' he commanded, pointing to Baz. Whisper realised his master was ahead of him, hiding underneath an old oak tree. He recognised Baz, even in the darkness. Whisper bounded up to him. A whistle went up and then quiet. Baz patted Whisper, letting him frolic a little before quietening him down to retrieve the message around his neck. *Ceasefire until 22:00 hours* read the message. Corporal Peters stealthily caught up with the soldier master and his dog.

'They have given us a two hour reprieve to retreat without fire!' stated Baz.

Corporal Peters was as shocked as Baz was. They had thought their best option was to keep going all the way to the fort and try their best to fire at as many men as they could. At least trying to make their way to the end of the underground tunnel. If they had been thinking clearly, with more sleep and more men they would have been faster, giving them a better chance to defeat the enemy. But if not for the ceasefire, the vulnerable battalion would surely have been shot dead or captured. Now they had the chance to run back to safe ground, over No Man's Land without being set upon and hounded. They were on a no win mission, but now they had won back their lives all thanks to Whisper charming the Germans and saving all of the men from the second Essex battalion that night.

Baz and Corporal Peters felt it was now or never to retreat and return to base camp. The whistle blew and all of the men followed Corporal Peters and Baz out through the woods to No Man's Land. Running over pitted mounds, and twigs and branches crunching underfoot, they reached the open ground and ran with all their might. Whisper led with Baz, his tongue lolling to one side. He was exhausted from his last run but kept on going at the heels of Baz, keeping one eye on the kite which was still circling overhead. Baz imagined the headlines of the newspaper as he ran - *Essex battalion saved by a messenger dog called Whisper. Two-hour ceasefire for Essex battalion who had time to re-group with army relief coming just in time. Well done Whisper!'*

CHAPTER 6 – HOMEWARD BOUND

The next day, Baz sat by the river Meuse with Whisper at his feet. Baz had taken his boots off and was dangling his feet in the cold water. He was exhausted and tonight, he and Whisper were invited to the Officers' Mess to relax, play cards and drink rum with the higher-ranking soldiers. There was talk too of Whisper being a hero. A journalist was looking to do a story on Whisper and his dog handler Baz Callum. Whisper's paw was bound now where he had cut it running for his life. Baz knew they would be sent home on leave, and he was happy for that. He felt they had had a lucky escape and his intuition told him he wouldn't necessarily get a second chance of luck out here. He needed to get Whisper home for now. The river was running high today. Not a cold day, and a welcome breeze came in gradually. Baz smiled as Whisper lifted his head to welcome it and lick his lips as if tasting the air. He looked relaxed to be with his soldier master by the river. He was used to the water. It felt like home.

'Excuse me Sir, may I sketch you and your dog?' a man asked. Obviously an artist, he had been watching Baz and Whisper for quite a while as he sat under a lime tree with his sketchpad. 'My name is Muirhead Bone and I am sketching some war scenes. I heard the story about your dog. May I sketch you now or later?'

Baz recognised the war artist from earlier on in the week. Muirhead had been accompanying the Essex battalion for a while now. His charcoal drawings had produced quite a following from the soldiers.[2]

'I'm Baz Callum and this is my messenger dog Whisper. Pleased to meet you,' he smiled, offering his hand to the young soldier. 'Yes of course you can sketch us, but we need to report to the Corporal now. Maybe tonight you could sketch us in the Officers' Mess. Come and join us for a glass of rum, but you may need to get some permission first,' he informed Muirhead.

'Oh they know me. It will be fine. I will see you a little later then,' said the artist.

Whisper let out a little whine and licked his bandaged paw. 'We're going home soon Whisper, I promise. Back to Three Shells Beach with Ryan, Jack and Vivien.'

Baz thought about Vivien, Ryan's older sister. He had met her briefly by the fishing boats when she came to find Ryan as he was saying goodbye to Whisper. How sweet she was. How pretty she was. Her curly brown hair framing her pretty heart shaped face. She was younger than Baz by a few years and he knew she had a boyfriend. Did she still, he wondered. 'What do you think of Vivien then, Whisper?' Baz asked his dog jokingly. Whisper put his snout on his paws and looked up and then down, glancing first at Baz and then at his paw. He looked as if he was rolling his eyes

---

[2] Muirhead Bone - Official War Artist 1876-1953

at his soldier master. It made Baz laugh. 'Come on then boy. Let's get you your dinner and then we can relax with the soldiers.' Whisper jumped up and then let out a little whimper. His leg was clearly still hurting him.

The Officer's Mess

A quiet ease fell upon the Officer's Mess. A game of cards was being quietly played out in the corner. There were maps spread out, mugs of cocoa and glasses of rum on the overcrowded table. A group of men from the Royal Flying Corps had joined the Essex battalion that night. Baz had struck up a friendship with an airman called Leonard Hosey who had been flying with the Canadian Air Corps all week but had joined the Essex battalion that evening. His best friend Paul Myers was a Royal Engineer with the gunners who had supposedly been meeting up with the Essex battalion a week ago. Leonard had landed his biplane the night before in Faubourg Pave' airfield, near Verdun. He then reported to the Officer's Mess that evening. He found out that Paul was missing in action. Leonard was going to spend tomorrow looking for him and then he would have to return to England on a mission.

'I'm sorry about your best friend,' said Baz empathetically.

'It's a strange one. He hasn't been heard of since Fort Vaux. But no one reported him missing. They say there was a captured German Maxin machine gun. Maybe that's where they got him. I know he was near the area.'

'Have you spoken to people that knew him out here?' asked Baz as Whisper let out a sigh and nuzzled into his lap.

'Yes but they thought he had left on leave and someone else said he was being called up for desertion! But something's not right. We go back along way and I just know he wouldn't disappear without a trace, unless he's been captured.'

Just then Corporal Maxwell Peters invited the men to sit at the Officer's Mess table to have something to eat. The men rose and Whisper slipped off Baz's lap and followed the men to sit with them. The men roared with laughter as Whisper jumped up and sat himself down next to the Corporal, snuggling up between the men as if waiting patiently for his meal.

'Whisper, get down!' Baz commanded, but he too could see the funny side. Whisper was becoming so popular he was getting too big for his boots! As the men sipped their rum, they enjoyed friendly banter between each other.

Leonard turned to Baz and said 'You know if you are looking to get home soon, I could fly you and your dog to Kent in the next couple of days.'

'Really?' said Baz, letting out a slow whistle. I have never been in a biplane. Would it be possible for Whisper?' he asked, rather concerned not for himself but for Whisper.

While they talked they could see the artist Muirhead Bone being introduced to the Flying Corps. Then he retreated quietly with his sketchpad in the corner of the room, just drawing and listening to the gentlemen's conversation. The dim light of the gas lamps casted a fog of mystery over the men, their plans and the room.

'Well I was thinking of leaving the day after tomorrow so what we can do is set off early. We can try Whisper on your lap and put a blanket over him, or he could sit at your feet but he would have to keep quite still. It would be a problem if he moves about but he seems well trained and obedient no doubt,' explained Leonard.

'Then I think he will be fine. He senses danger. He's sensible. He wouldn't put us in danger,' retorted Baz knowing Whisper could be depended on.

> *The ancient fortress City of Verdun*
>
> *That sits by the river Meuse,*
>
> *Our troops and allies - our Essex*
>
> *Worked hard not to loose.*

*

The following day after Baz's interview with a war correspondent for the Evening Standard in London, he nursed Whisper's paw in the cool of the water in the river. He kissed his soft fur on his head and soothed him as he splashed the liquid around the sore paw. 'There Whisper, we will soon be fit for home,' said Baz reassuringly. Whisper wagged his tail enthusiastically. He was ready. Ready for anything again with his soldier master. Baz had received word from Leonard to meet him tomorrow near the airfield in Faubourg Pave' where his Curtiss Jenny Biplane was being looked after by some American troops. The men decided the best and safest way to transport Whisper would be to put him on Baz's lap for the whole of the flight. It was too much of a risk to put Whisper at his feet and if he moved or fell it would be catastrophic.

Bracing himself as the engine started, Baz felt the beads of perspiration slip down his forehead. The men had wrapped Whisper in a blanket and placed a soft helmet on his head with goggles. He didn't seem to mind. Baz only hoped they would take off gracefully with the plane coping with the weight of the two other passengers. Leonard had reassured him that as Baz was slight in build then it should not be a problem. The only problem they could have now was if Whisper took fright and started to move about. Baz buried his head into Whisper's neck as they took off, with the little aeroplane juddering noisily along the grassy runway which seemed to take an incredibly long amount of time until they swiftly took off. The exhilaration was incredible and to Baz's surprise, even Whisper seemed to enjoy it with his head now peeping out of the blanket and his ears flapping in the wind. 'Good boy Whisper,' he said as they soared into the sky overlooking copses and forests. The loud buzzing of the aircraft was disconcerting to say the least but soon they both adjusted to it. Leonard gave them the thumbs up as they swung left over to what Baz presumed was the Channel. Blue below them and blue above them. Baz was feeling disorientated, clinging to Whisper who seemed braver then himself! Baz looked out and imagined that this is what the kite would see from this height, soaring across the sky, watching the waves and what seemed like tiny boats in the distance. The time just flew by and before they knew it they were coming down to land. Baz could see the White Cliffs of Dover and then he saw lines of trees and houses and after a little while, they lowered even more. Some slight turbulence made the plane shake as they began their descent into an airfield.

'Welcome to Kent Boys!' shouted Leonard as they came to an abrupt stop. Some fellow airmen who had been running to keep up with the plane caught up with them to have a look at Whisper.

'Home Whisper,' said Baz. Whisper barked back.

CHAPTER 7 – THE REUNION

Baz opened the letter from Jack Leemer. A lump in his throat made him cough. Whisper stirred in his sleep on Baz's bed at the Coggeshall Barracks. His snout rising up and down as it rested on Baz's boots. His handsome face had a look of peaceful contentment. His paw was improving daily and now he was out of pain. He was a happy dog again, but for one thing. 'Where was Ryan?' he thought. Baz began to read the letter. It read:

June 10th 1916

Dear Mr Callum

I hope this letter finds you in good health. I sent it to the Coggeshall Barracks as I know you will be returning to England fairly soon. I hesitated to send it all the way to France.

I implore you Mr Callum, on your return you visit us here at Three Shells Beach. Unfortunately Mrs Kelly has passed away and Ryan is devastated. If on your return you can come and bring Whisper, Ryan would love it as his spirits are low and he misses that dog. As you can imagine there is only a certain amount I can do. An old coot like me can do little to cheer up the young lad. His sister Vivien is worried about his schoolwork and I haven't seen him read for a while. He was so diligent with his studies, which have faltered, and his ambition to go to a good college to become a teacher seems so distant now. I ask him about it and he says he doesn't want to think about it at all. I fear his ambition has gone to the back of his mind.

We are all worried for him as his stepfather pushes him to become an oyster fisherman. They fish most days and I watch them go out in the morning. Same routine with their blue nets and same clothes. Ryan pushes the boat out as his stepfather barks orders. Of course the sea air is good for him and he is healthy but quiet and compliant where his stepfather is concerned. I know he sketches the scenes of the sea and he shows me a few of them. He draws the kites, the Redshanks and the Godwits which are quite remarkable. It would be nice for him to have Whisper here for him to draw when he gets back.

Please visit us. I hope that this doesn't trouble you at your barracks and upset your privacy but we need to do something quickly. I don't like to gossip either but I have seen his stepfather clip him around the ear a few times and I feel if Don Kelly sees a few of us watching, maybe he won't pick on the boy so much.

Hope to see you and Whisper soon

Kind Wishes

Jack Leemer

Baz looked at his pocket watch. It was too late to go to Three Shells Beach tonight. It was passed seven o' clock, but he had a few days leave so he decided to start out early tomorrow. Maybe a few days for him and Whisper by the sea again would do them the world of good too. Whisper could benefit from the salt on his wound. The cuts had healed but he was still limping. The cool of the sea would help him. Maybe, he thought, he could go fishing with Ryan. He had never been oyster fishing before. It would take Ryan's mind off things and he would be happy to see Whisper again.

An Oyster an Oyster,

A pearl amongst the grit,

Grin and bear it, this life

Against the enemy.

We will rise above the sea,

Us Essex are worth our salt

That flows through our waters,

And through our veins – our Blighty.

We will conquer all thoughts of a threat.

*

July 1916

Ryan had returned to school today. Don Kelly was not

pleased about it. Not at all. But his sister Vivien had put her foot down with her stepfather, and with the backing of Doctor Partridge he had agreed to let him see out the summer term and take his English Literature exam that day.

Later Ryan sat on Three Shells beach. It had been a hot day and still warm, even at four o' clock in the afternoon. The sun was still beating down on the waters. The tide had turned and as it shone on the twinkling sea. Ryan could see the kite had returned as it was sitting on a green fishing boat, spying on Ryan as Ryan spied upon it. Then all of a sudden it took flight. Its wings outstretched and it flew off in the direction of what Ryan thought must be France. He wondered if their houses were like his – a stone and white washed cottage. Feeling hungry, he wondered what the French food was like. He sighed and picked at the sea grass. Its long stems forcing Ryan to tug at them hard to pull them out at the roots. He kicked the sand as he stood up. He placed his dirty hands in his pockets. Jack Leemer was making tea in his kitchen and he had been watching the boy from his window. Making the snap decision to ask the boy if he wanted a cup, he shouted at Ryan who had already begun to run. Counting the minutes in his head, Ryan didn't hear Jack. 'One minute… two minutes… I will be home in four minutes,' he thought. Jack Leemer shook his head. He hoped Baz and Whisper would come soon.

The next day Don Kelly insisted that they work on the boat as his exams were over. A storm had blown in early last night. Possibly from France, pondered Don Kelly. But it had taken hold of the little fishing village and some of the boats had been destroyed and wooden decking from the jetty had taken a beating. Jack Leemer was up early, tying some string around two planks of wood, temporarily keeping them together until he could get some other men to help him. He had made a notice for people to warn them not to go on the jetty until he had repaired it. The old man was using his hammer to beat a nail into a wooden post to place the warning. The wind was still rough but he could hear voices behind him.

'Look, our boat's still intact,' said Don Kelly, nudging Ryan roughly by his elbow. He could see their little blue fishing boat bob about in the sea. 'Aye, if you're a good fisherman you should always look after your boat. No sea, swirl or harbinger can destroy it if you take care of your Oyster Catcher!'

Ryan looked to see if he could see the kite today. It wasn't around. He hoped it had survived the storm. Then a thought took hold of him. 'Whisper. What if he wasn't alive? Where was Whisper and Baz?' He wanted to cry but bit his lip. He felt sick and wanted to be anywhere but with his stepfather today.

'Morning,' said Jack Leemer to Don Kelly as they passed under the jetty to seek their boat.

'Morning,' replied Don Kelly gruffly, hating the old man that seemed to spend too much time with his stepson. Ryan couldn't meet Jack Leemer's eyes. He would cry if he did.

'I don't suppose you two could help me with the jetty? I just need two men to help tie these last posts together,' Jack asked.

'Sorry Jack but we're busy today. You're sure to find someone else,' Don Kelly snapped back at him. Ryan looked in Jacks direction again and the old man could see a look of desperation on his face.

'That man was despicable,' thought Jack to himself. Just then, as they were about to go under the jetty, they heard a loud whistle. Ryan turned around and to his delight he could see a dog running along the beach. Was it Whisper? Could it be him? he thought. His face lit up in anticipation. Sure enough, he saw a man in a soldier's uniform and a black and white terrier running towards him. Ryan waved his arms over his head trying to catch the dog's attention. Don Kelly shouted at Ryan to stop but Ryan was determined to catch the dog's eye. Suddenly the terrier stopped in his tracks. He looked down the bank of sand and recognised the boy. He set off again leaving a trail of sand behind him, barking furiously with Baz in hot pursuit. The dog bounded up to Ryan who was already crouching, waiting for the dog to jump into his arms. Whisper was quite a large dog but he still leapt in the air with all his might. Ryan laughed as he caught him and they both fell backwards into the dunes. Whisper licked his face as if Ryan was his favourite meal. Baz was running towards them now. Don Kelly just watched with irritation, scratching his head and sighing loudly. Keen to set sail, he turned his back on the boy and continued wading into the shallows to get to his blue boat.

'Whisper I have missed you,' Ryan cried as he buried his face into the dog's warm fur around his neck. Whisper continued to bark and was now running rings around the boy, his tail wagging nineteen to the dozen, his tongue lolling like it always did when he was hot.

'Be quiet Whisper,' shouted Baz catching up with them. Jack Leemer just stood and watched the happy reunion. He placed his tools down on the wooden decking, walked back down the jetty and made his way onto the beach towards the foray of noise.

'So pleased you made it here today, my friend. You must have received my letter.' Jack smiled warmly.

'I did,' replied Baz now shaking the old man's hand.

'And the war. How did it treat you?' said Jack now watching Baz and Ryan hug. He wasn't sure but he thought he could see a tear of joy run down Ryan's face. Smiling, Jack could see Don Kelly set sail, realising he had lost Ryan's attention for the day.

'Your stepfather is going without you,' warned Jack.

'I don't care,' replied Ryan defiantly.

'Maybe you should go. We'll wait for you to return,' said Baz realising it wouldn't be worth his act of defiance against Don Kelly.

Ryan thought for a moment. Baz was right and besides, he thought, in a couple of hours they would be back. His stepfather had mentioned he had to meet a friend in the early afternoon.

'Will you still be here this afternoon?' Ryan asked, imploring them to stay as his huge brown eyes now lit up with happiness at the thought of it.

'Of course,' replied Baz, giving the boy a reassuring squeeze on the shoulder as he turned and waded into the water after the little blue boat. 'We will stay until you get back. Don't worry.'

Ryan sat on the edge of the boat watching Whisper barking at him by the shore. Ryan's stepfather was barking orders at him. 'Pass me the knives in the black bag please. Hurry with the sail. What are you doing over there? You know you need to be this side,' he demanded.

Ryan turned his attention to the job in hand, now knowing he had a reason to be happy to return to shore in only a couple of hours. Ryan picked up the oysters which were being hauled into the boat, carefully choosing the ones that would make the grade, and sizing the ones he wasn't sure about through the hoop. Woe betide him if he made a mistake. Throwing a few back, and then pulling at the net, he looked at Don Kelly who seemed miles away now in his own thoughts. His leathery weather beaten skin made him look older than his years. His tobacco stained fingers played in the knotted rope, making Ryan feel distinctly uneasy. His hair still full but grey at the temples and there were deep lines of worry on his forehead. He had been handsome in his youth, but not now. Anger had made him age and the corners of his mouth drooped downward. He only seemed happy when he menacingly picked on Ryan. Ryan was sure he thought of him like an unwelcome spat. Too small to keep but he just couldn't bring himself to throw the boy away. He just toyed with him like a bird of prey pecking at its small morsel to eat. Ryan was sure that the highlight of Don Kelly's day had been picking on him and his mother until he went to work.

'What you starting at, you weird one?' Don shouted at Ryan.

'Nothing,' Ryan replied, startled Don Kelly had caught him staring.

'Look! That damn kite is back, circling us again. Always after our oysters,' he spat.

At that moment the kite took a dive down to the boat and knocked Don Kelly off balance, falling back into the netting and covering him in oyster shells. The bird picked up an oyster and flew off as quick as it had appeared. Ryan smirked. It didn't take too much to throw the man off balance. He had probably had a tank full of beer already, he thought. Don Kelly got to his feet embarrassed. He wouldn't have wanted Ryan to catch him in a weak moment. He lunged at the boy and swung at his head, striking his forehead with his fist. Ryan flew backwards.

'Watch yourself young Ryan,' smiled Don Kelly, happy he had inflicted pain on the young man.

Ryan stood up carefully. Dazed and furious, tears fell down his cheeks. How he hated his stepfather. A boat had quietly passed them and two men had seen Don Kelly strike Ryan. They had at first been watching the birds, but witnessed the argument between Ryan and Don Kelly. There were storm clouds overhead and the boat began to rock in the brackish water. It started to rain, and Don Kelly decided to call it a day. For the short sail back, Ryan didn't look at his stepfather at all, only passing him paraphernalia from the boat when he had to. Now he was not going to be submissive. Something had changed between them. Ryan felt stronger. This man could do no more harm now. It was Ryan that he had to be afraid of. Like a spat metamorphosing into an oyster, Ryan was changing from a boy to a man. His gut was now in tune with the rhythm of the sea. He knew how he was going to cope with this man. A pearl of wisdom was growing within him. Through sheer grit and determination his silvery armour was formed. No one would ever hit him again. His outer shell was impenetrable, and Don Kelly had better watch out.

Vivien was waiting for them on the jetty. She was worried about the weather and Jack Leemer had been warning other fisherman to make sure their boats were tightly secured to the pilings at the jetty.

'This is going to be one hell of a storm,' said Jack, warning the local fisherman out this morning.

Intense storm swirls were coming with vigorous
determination to wreak havoc on the fishing community
again. Relieved to see Ryan, she beckoned for him to get
out of the boat quickly. Vivien hugged her younger brother
as he made his way to the jetty to where she was standing.
He left Don Kelly to secure the rope to the piling. Ryan
wasn't going to help him. He really didn't give a damn
about him now. She saw the welt on his forehead and
kissed his sweating brow.

'I have just seen Whisper,' she said, speaking softly into his
ear. 'Listen I will tell stepfather you have to come to the
shop with me and we can have half an hour with Whisper
and Baz at Jack Leemer's house. I saw you come in. I was
hoping you would finish the day early due to the storm
coming.'

Don Kelly was happy to see the back of Ryan for the day.
He was in as much rush to get into the village to see his
friend as Ryan was to see Whisper and Baz. The angry man
rushed up from the swirling waters, changed into his boots
and walked onto the sand dunes, leaving Three Shells
Beach.

'Let's celebrate,' said Jack as he opened a bottle of
champagne that had been left there at the cottage by his
brother before he set sail for Ireland last year.

'None for Ryan, Mr Leemer,' said Vivien firmly as the
adults clinked their glasses at Whisper and Baz.

'Do you think you will be going back to the Western Front

Mr Callum?' asked Vivien, interested in this young soldier who had taken such good care of Whisper.

'Me? Yes, definitely but not Whisper, at least for a while. He will need to recover. But please Vivien, call me Baz,' he stated, looking at the pretty girl.

Vivien blushed as she was aware of Baz staring at her longer than was necessary.

'But I am sure they will call me up again in the next month or two. I have to have medical checkups and as a dog handler, I am responsible for Whisper so it's my duty to hand over Whisper to someone suitable for the time being,' affirmed Baz, looking downcast.

Ryan listened intently. The thought of anyone else having Whisper was inconceivable.

'I wish I could take him,' started up Ryan with a bitterness in his voice.

'Well once they become a working dog, the army like them not to become domestic pets again, not whilst there is still working life left in them,' explained Baz.

'I see. That makes sense,' Jack said mulling over the situation.

Whisper breathed heavily by the fire. His eyes had begun to shut with tiredness until he had contentedly fallen asleep. Ryan thought he looked like a domestic pet all right. As he listened to the adults talk, he sat quietly sipping his tea and eating a scone that Jack had just heated up in the stove. An idea came to him. One that made him feel happy. Happier than he had been in a long time.

'We best be going Ryan,' said Vivien, aware that it was getting dark outside. 'We had better get to the shop before stepfather returns from the tavern.'

Ryan got up to go reluctantly. He went over to the still sleeping dog and hugged him around his neck. Whisper stirred, lifted his head and licked Ryan on the forehead.

'Can I see Whisper soon?' asked Ryan as Baz reached for his jacket by the door.

'Of course. As I said we will be back to Three Shells Beach soon. Maybe next week,' confirmed Baz. 'If that is all right with everyone?'

Jack smiled at Baz in agreement.

'Come on Whisper,' commanded Baz as the tired dog rose from the rug to leave. 'I will walk you to the village shop, Vivien,' said Baz, feeling self- conscious in her presence. He wanted to ask Vivien a question, and hoped she would say yes.

Jack Leemer shook the soldiers hand. 'See you next week,' he said, patting Whisper on top of his head.

It was a cool evening, and aware they had spent longer at Jack's house then they had intended, they walked at a quick pace. Ryan started to count the minutes.

'What did you say Ryan?' asked Baz as he thought he heard the young man ask him something. Baz and Vivien walked behind them now.

'Don't worry,' smiled Vivien to Baz. 'He always counts the time. Just aware not to be late, that's all.'

Baz's brow furrowed. He wondered what life was like for these two living with that man Don Kelly now that their mother had gone.

Ryan reached the shop first and before Vivien could go in, Baz caught her arm gently. 'I was just wondering when I'm back next week, may I take you to the picture house?'

Vivien's eyes lit up. She liked this soldier with his unfamiliar accent. 'I would like that very much thank you, but usually I am only free on a Wednesday. It's our stepfather's day off then so he is usually in the tavern most of the day. He's usually not concerned about where I am then. It just makes life easier. I won't have to cook for him. Not that he likes my cooking though,' she said with a wry smile at Baz.

'Great. That would be perfect for us. I will put in a days leave and maybe, if the weather is nice, you, me, Ryan and Whisper can have a picnic first together?' Baz asked.

'Ryan has Jack tutor him on a Wednesday evening so that would be fine. Thank you, Baz. I shall look forward to it,' she said, re-opening the shop door. Baz rushed off with Whisper so full of confidence he even forgot to say goodbye to Ryan again.

As Vivien waved to Baz, she went up to pick up a basket by the counter. 'Is your stepfather going to enlist?' enquired Mr Ferry, the shopkeeper, to Vivien as he reached for the key to close up shop.

'I have no idea Mr Ferry. I didn't know they were asking for more men to go out to the Western Front yet,' responded Vivien.

'Well I think they are recruiting even older men now,' said Mr Ferry, aware Ryan was listening. He didn't want to say the word 'deceased' about the younger soldiers. 'So many soldiers have lost their lives now.'

'I was thinking of enlisting, Mr Ferry,' said Ryan boldly.

'You will do no such thing,' said Vivien sharply at Ryan. 'You are not sixteen yet.'

'I am soon,' he stated, looking at Mr Ferry directly in the eye.

'Ryan, just pass me that box of eggs would you,' said Vivien coldly, trying to change the subject.

'I saw your stepfather with Carole Maloney earlier. She steals from me you know,' said Mr Ferry, expecting some explanation from Vivien.

'Well I am sorry about that Mr Ferry, but who my stepfather chooses to spend his time with is nothing to do with me,' responded Vivien imperiously.

Mr Ferry glanced down through his spectacles at the heavy basket of food, aware that he had perhaps said too much in front of Ryan. When they left the shop Vivien couldn't help but feel annoyed. Everyone knew Don Kelly had been seeing Carole Maloney behind her mothers back for years and now he was openly flaunting the women. She hated him now. Even perhaps more than Ryan did.

'Who is Carole Maloney, Viv?' asked Ryan with his hands in his pockets.

'Oh no one. Just a friend of our stepfathers,' she replied awkwardly.

Ryan pursed his lips. How could anyone want to be a friend of stepfather he thought as they walked through the grey front door of their little white stone cottage. Don Kelly had his boots up on the table and eyed the pair with suspicion as they ignored him and went about their business.

CHAPTER 8 – RETURN TO WAR

SEPTEMBER 1916

Baz was missing Whisper. He wondered how Ryan, Vivien and Jack were getting on at Three Shells Beach. He had been in France for two months now and was firmly entrenched in the battle of Delville Wood, Longueval. He was feeling battle weary. The Essex battalion were exhausted. Their first mission had been to clear Delville Wood of as many German soldiers as they could but it hadn't been an easy task. Fighting alongside them were the South African Brigade who had lost so many men. They had been constantly interrupted by mud and rainwater which hindered their advancement. Baz wanted to go home. One more week out here and he would be on his way home... if he survived.

*

The wild geese had returned from Canada. Ryan would listen to the hooping and haunting noises that they would make as they flew overhead. It created an eerie atmosphere that made Ryan feel uncomfortable. Ryan watched as the geese jostled for position, forming a v-shape underneath the clouds in the early morning dawn. Flapping their wings and honking noisily, they flew towards the village.

The weather had turned at Three Shells Beach. The autumnal season had set upon them. It was cold at night and Vivien insisted that the fire be kept alight even when Don Kelly said they didn't have the money to waste on firewood. Ryan was sent out to find driftwood before school every morning and sometimes Jack would walk with him with Whisper at their heels. It was enough time for the two of them to talk about the latest books they were both reading. Ryan would gather the rough pieces of wood in a basket and he would walk slowly home, his arms aching, feeling as if they would come out of their sockets at any moment. Sometimes he would pull the basket with a piece of rope that Jack had found for him, especially if it was a particularly heavy load. The driftwood would dry out during the day ready for the evening where Vivien and Ryan would place it in the small open fire. Sitting by it, Ryan would read and Vivien would knit. She loved knitting and hoped one day to have her own shop. Sometimes she would sell her children's sweaters at the local market on Saturday's after she closed the Post Office at lunchtime. Her babies booties were really popular too. Tonight she had started a new blue pair for the neighbours little boy Fred. His father George had just been injured in the war, and was still in France. It was a worrying time for the little family and he hadn't even met his baby boy yet. Vivien thought the booties would make a nice gift for the baby. Don Kelly was late in from the tavern. However, as it was a Wednesday, the pair were not surprised and was actually something they looked forward to. A bit of peace and quiet before he came home was welcome until the inevitable bullying and arguing occurred between them, with Don Kelly generally being provocative to start a disagreement. As Vivien began to start on the second bootie, she looked at the clock on the mantle piece and realised it was later than she thought. He was not normally this late. Yawning, she told Ryan that it would be best if he went to bed now as Don Kelly would be home soon.

'Let's not give him a reason to be angry with us,' she said wisely, pursing her lips.

Kissing his sister on her cheek, Ryan ran upstairs and jumped into bed. He knew Don Kelly's temper was getting worse each day. He expected him to be home any second and counted the minutes one by one until he fell asleep. Stoking the fire again and deciding to wait up for her stepfather, Vivien sat in her mother's rocking chair continuing to knit. Out of the corner of her eye she could see the moon through the large window by the door. It shone brightly, making the sea light up and a white mist descended on the small patch of water below it. The sea was black tonight and the water underneath the moon looked like a little island. Something else caught her eye and she rose from her chair. Putting down her knitting, she watched a small fishing boat glide along in the unusual stillness of the water. Under the moon it slunk along suspiciously. She couldn't see who was in it and it puzzled her. Normally no one fished at this time. It was a very disturbing sight, she thought, as she wondered if it could be a foreign boat. She thought perhaps Jack Leemer had seen it too as he was always watching the sea. But perhaps he was asleep now as it was so late, she thought.

It was midnight now and still no sign of Don Kelly. He had talked about enlisting yesterday. More men were needed at the Western Front and some of the older men were being asked to go now. Vivien was aware in the past that Don Kelly had not wanted to go to France before and had used an excuse of having an injured leg from a boating accident years ago. All of a sudden he seemed awfully keen to go. She guessed it was because his girlfriend Carole Maloney was having his baby. She hadn't told Ryan this news. Don Kelly didn't want anyone else to know but there was talk in the village. Everyone knew everyone else's business. Typical of him, Vivien thought, he would escape responsibility this way. She remembered he said he was going into town to be measured for a uniform but that was at lunchtime. He was a creature of habit. She thought about walking along the beach to Jack Leemer's house to tell him and to alert him about the suspicious fishing boat she had seen earlier but she thought better of it. Instead she locked the door and shuddered. She didn't feel safe. She put away her knitting in the basket by the front door and blew out the two candles that were nearly down to their wicks. Tomorrow she would inform the home guard if Don Kelly hadn't appeared.

A week later as Baz was preparing to leave France, he reported to his Officer in charge, Lieutenant Conner McNamara. Conner was someone the men got on with very well. He was great fun and not at all stuffy like some of the other officers he had served with during his time in the Essex battalion since the beginning of the war. His father was Irish but had moved to a village near Colchester called Brightlingsea, a fishing village similar to Three Shells Beach, to start a new life with his family. There were many Irish immigrants that had moved to England in the last few years before the war. Connor was praised for getting on well with the Australian and New Zealand soldiers that were training with the Essex battalion because of the similar terrain to the Western Front. It was a testing time for all of Britain. Nobody's lives were improving. Conner McNamara knew how to survive. Shot once in the arm last year, he had saved two men from certain death by lying on them to protect them mid- battle. His arm stretched across one man's head, taking the full force of the bullet. He had received the Military Cross for that. Everyone looked up to him.

Now one man in particular, his friend Leonard Hosey, was to be honoured for his flying and journalistic abilities. Reporting to his friend Lieutenant Conner McNamara, he had flown in from Kent that morning to meet up with the Essex battalion. Baz had just finished all of his military duties and was ready to be put on leave. He decided to ask Leonard Hosey if he could fly back to Kent the following day with him.

'How are you, my good friend,' said Leonard to Baz, patting him on the back. 'No Whisper this time?' he inquired.

'No I'm afraid not. He was injured and although healed now, he is still resting with friends in Essex,' explained Baz, wistfully thinking about his loyal dog. 'Is it possible for you to fly me back if you're returning tomorrow to Kent?'

'I will fly you back by all means but this afternoon I would like to visit the American hospital where my good friend Paul Meyers has been found at long last,' responded Leonard.

'That's good news! Where is this military hospital?' asked Baz, smiling and feeling happy for the kind pilot.

'It's in Amineres. You could come with me. We can stay back from enemy lines in a little village I know near the aerodrome and then continue our journey tomorrow back to Kent. Some of the Canadian boys at the hospital will be pleased to see a fellow Canadian visit them,' explained the Lieutenant.

'Sounds perfect to me. Let me get my permission to leave and I will be back with you in the hour,' replied Baz, excited to be going home.

It was Sunday and a week had gone by since Don Kelly had disappeared. Vivien and Ryan sat on the decking outside their cottage together. Whisper was at Ryan's feet. Vivien had relented and let Whisper stay with them. It was clear Don Kelly was not returning. There was nothing to be afraid of except she wanted to know the truth about what had befallen him. She had taken the day off work yesterday to go to Billingsgate Market in London to search for him. On the day that he had disappeared Vivien had found out through a local man called Billy McKenzie that apparently he was seen there selling his Friday catch of oysters a week ago. If he really needed the money Don Kelly would normally go up to the market on a Friday or Saturday every few months but lately it hadn't been so frequent due to his excessive drinking.

'I could swear it was him. He even waved to me from the far side of the market. He was wearing the same cap and jacket that he always wears,' explained Billy.

'But surely he would have told me he was going,' said Vivien wondering if this man had made a mistake.

'Look I could be wrong, but I never mistake a face. But he was with someone I didn't recognise though,' retorted Billy.

'Really?' asked Vivien intrigued. 'Don Kelly had few friends. Who was he with?'

'An older man of about seventy. He had a walking stick and looked like he was in pain when he walked. They were sitting down by the entrance of the market and then they got up. Don waved to me and he helped this older man to his feet and they went about their business. Disappeared. I didn't see them again. That's all I can tell you really,' admitted the local.

'Well he didn't return home that evening. But thank you for telling me,' Vivien said, perplexed.

Vivien stroked Whisper's face. 'Don't suppose *you,* Mr Whisper, will be going back to War. Look at you all domesticated,' she said playfully, then planting a kiss on the back of his head as the dog lay contentedly by their feet. Ryan sighed, looking up to his sister.

'What are we going to do Sis? About money I mean?' he asked, his brow starting to furrow. He stood up on the deck and looked out to Jack Leemer's house across the beach. His hair was a mess from the continuing strong winds from the latest storm. Some of the sea defences had been battered this week and some military police and home guard were busy fixing them today. A seagull was picking at a dropped oyster shell a few feet away and Whisper watched the bird with intensity, his brown eyes barely blinking as he stared at the gull with interest and amusement.

Vivien stood up and put her arm around her younger brother's shoulders. 'You let me worry about that. I could do another shift at the post office. Mr Ferry seemed annoyed with me yesterday though for taking the day off. He said he didn't need any extra help in the store so that's not an option. But don't worry, I will look for a second shift somewhere else if possible as the rent is due soon. So Ryan it's not your concern,' she assured him. 'You have your studies to work hard for. You wanted to become a teacher didn't you?' she asked, trying to soothe him. Vivien knew him to be vulnerable and sullen these days and she just wanted to comfort him. Everything she said to him was measured not wanting to overly upset him. She knew he wasn't over his mother's death.

Ryan shrugged. 'Come on Whisper, let's go and see Jack.' Ryan started to walk off with Whisper who was quick to come to heel and take off with his master to Jack's house.

Biting on the inside of her lip she watched her brother walk quickly along the beach. Tears stung her eyes. Whisper's ears flew back in the strong winds and she knew he would be blinking back the salty spray from his eyes and licking his salty nose. She loved them both and wished she could bring their lives back to normality. This war had taken a toll on everything and everyone around them, she thought. She feigned a smile when in the distance he turned and waved to her. Waving back she then turned to go inside the cottage. It was getting colder in the evenings now and while fetching her stole she was surprised when she heard a knock at the door. A man in uniform stood in front of her. Startled, her first thoughts were of Baz and his safety.

'Sorry to trouble you Ma'am. I am Sergeant Ted Ferris, from the Home Guard. I need to speak to you. A body has been found and I do believe it maybe your stepfather.'

Vivien lent back in shock, and steadied herself with a chair as she felt her head swim.

'You had better sit down,' he recommended. 'Have you something to drink in the house? Can I make you a cup of tea or something stronger?' he asked, worried by the ghostly look on her face. She had paled and she really thought she may faint.

'Please will you shut the door. The wind is blowing sand into the house.' she said wearily. The Sergeant did as she asked. Seating himself down next to her he took out his note book.

'Would you be willing to identify him? His friend Billy McKenzie says it's him but we found the body without a coat on. No wallet or identification.'

'I don't know,' Vivien said, feeling overwhelmed with what this man was telling her. 'Could you perhaps ask Jack Leemer to do it? I'm not sure I'm up to it. He knew him well enough.'

'Right you are missy,' replied the Sergeant, now getting up to look for the kettle to make some tea.

'Where did you find him?' she asked. 'He has been missing for just over a week now,' she said, starting to cry with shock.

Pouring hot water into the teapot, he paused and then looked Vivien straight into the eyes and said 'Inside one of the disused rowing boats I'm afraid. It looks like foul play to me. He had a deep cut on his forehead.'

'I see,' she replied.

'Is it correct that you reported a fishing boat out sailing the other night?' he asked, placing the teapot on the table and now beginning to look for his pen in his inside pocket.

'Yes that's right. I thought it suspicious at the time,' she said, now dabbing her eyes with her handkerchief.

'Well we have a reason to believe it could be some foreign stowaways that could have harmed him. Of course we may never find out. There are so many strange and unpredictable things happening right now. Most of our young men have gone to fight in France. But with so few men around, anybody we don't recognize sticks out like a sore thumb in the village.' Flipping through his notepad, he explained that these men barely talked in the tavern but when they did it was in a whisper. 'Someone overheard this and reported them. It was a young lady apparently. They had bothered her one evening and so she sensibly took action.'

Vivien look up inquisitively, 'Do you mind if I ask the lady's name?'

Looking through his notes Ted found the women's name. 'A Carole Maloney,' he responded.

'That was his girlfriend. How awful,' Vivien gasped.

'Well there you go then. Maybe it was a tit for tat thing. Sorry to be so blunt but case closed I think,' said the Sergeant with a down to earth tone to his voice.

Vivien wiped her eyes and, feeling better after the tea, got up to check the time. 'My brother is with Mr Leemer right now. Maybe we could go over together to his cottage? He will know what to do in the circumstances,' she said, pulling on her stole and opening the front door. A fresh gust of wind blew in, but instead of shivering she felt a renewed energy. Don Kelly was gone. There was no reason to be unhappy anymore.

CHAPTER 9 – NEW PLANS

Three weeks later

Life had returned to normal. Ryan seemed more cheerful and although he had left school, Jack Leemer was tutoring him on Wednesday and Friday evenings. Vivien, although struggling financially, was working two evenings a week in the local tavern, and getting out more had made her happy. Instead of having the uncomfortable watchful eyes of Don Kelly on them both, Ryan and Vivien were free to come and go as they pleased. Ryan rarely counted his minutes as he used to when his stepfather was alive. Even Vivien had made new friends, a few local girls from Coggeshall who were working alongside her. One girl, Evelyn, had a fiancé out in France and like Baz, he was in the Essex battalion. She had told Vivien that he was returning in a few days and she was looking forward to seeing him.

'Had any more letters from your friend Baz?' she asked.

Vivien shook her head. She had been thinking about him lately and his last letter was three or so weeks ago. He had mentioned he would be home soon so she presumed it would be in the next few days.

'I think he will be returning with your fiancé Mark, then,' she continued.

Thinking on it, she was surprised now that Jack Leemer hadn't mentioned any word from Baz. There had been so many changes in the last few weeks, she hadn't given Baz's return much thought. She had presumed no news was good news. Now she had a lump in her throat with fear. Something didn't sit right with her. She would pick up Ryan tonight on her way back from her shift at the White Lion tavern and talk to Jack to see if he'd received a letter and forgotten to mention it. As she walked hurriedly beside Three Shells Beach, along the coastal road that led to the coastguard's house she felt some eyes on her. Looking to her left in the semi-darkness, she saw the kite's yellow eyes fixed on her as it sat still on a post just staring at her as she passed by. But no sooner had she moved passed it, the bird took off into the dusk and flew over the beach. Swooping back along the road again it led the way to Jack's house. She could see Whisper in the sandy garden in front of the house, barking at the kite in the distance. The bird of prey came to rest on the flower pots by the house as Vivien rapped on the door.

'The kite's back. I haven't seen it for a while. It followed me here,' she reported.

'Aye, strange bird that,' said Jack looking rather worried.

'Everything all right?' asked Vivien, now rather spooked, looking around for Ryan in the sitting room.

'It's all right. He left a few minutes ago. You must have passed him on the coastal road did you not?' said Jack, relieved to see Vivien.

'No I did not. Oh my goodness Mr Leemer, where is he? What made him go home knowing I was picking him up? It's quite dark outside. He knows I like to come here and collect him when it's late,' she cried, her face paling.

'Come let's go and look for him. I am sure he hasn't gone far. You see we had words. I was just trying to soothe a situation,' explained the coastguard.

'What situation?' she asked.

'He has been talking about going out to France with Whisper. You know he wants to train as a dog handler. Whisper's handler,' informed Jack.

'No Jack, I had no idea. When did this all start up?' she said looking startled. 'He is nearly sixteen. He is far too young is he not? Do you think he's gone home?' she said, starting to panic.

'You don't think he would leave without that dog do you?' said Jack, trying to assure Vivien.

'No, no of course not. I see your point.' she said, suddenly feeling relieved that the possibility of him disappearing to France or anywhere else without Whisper was an unlikely scenario. Whisper was sitting by the fire now, his ears down and his tail between his legs looking despondent.

'Look there's no need to panic. I am sure he has just gone for a walk to calm down. I gave him quite a talking to and told him not to be silly. Let me fetch my coat,' said Jack, reaching for his heavy jacket from the back of the chair.

'Come on boy, let's find Ryan,' Jack instructed Whisper as they reached the front door.

Ryan was kicking the sand up as he walked. The kite was overhead, swooping down to pick up some shells and then taking off, wings outstretched and then finally heading out over the sea. The sea was howling tonight and the spray was vicious. Jack and Vivien shielded their eyes as they reached the shore with Whisper barking in front of them. The dog had caught up with Ryan first as he sat by their old fishing boat, sheltering from the spray. Whisper licked his face. When Ryan's sister caught up with him she threw her arms around him.

'Stop it, just stop it! Leave me alone!' he cried. 'Everyone!'

'What is it Ryan? What's the matter?' she asked, now starting to cry. Her hair mangled and strands of it blew into her mouth. She spat it out.

'It's everyone. Everyone treats me like a child but I'm not. I am a man now. Sixteen tomorrow and I need a job and I want to enlist alongside Baz and the other men in the battalion. I want to sign up and I am going to!' he shouted back to them.

'Ryan please let's go home. We can talk about this at home,' Vivien pleaded with him.

'If you don't agree with me I will take myself and Whisper off tonight to the barracks to train. I can you know. You don't have enough money for us Viv, I need to pay my way.'

'But not like this Ryan, really I can't lose you. Everything else is lost,' she cried.

Even their elder brother Josh had enlisted last week and was now in France. They hadn't seen him in a year and now he was out on the Western Front. Now Jack had put his arm around her protectively.

'Listen Ryan. Come back to my house with Whisper and we will discuss this in the morning,' said Jack, hoping he could persuade him.

'At least let me train with Whisper?' Ryan looked imploringly at the pair.

Jack shrugged and looked to Vivien. Exhausted, she had to agree to get him back inside the house and out of the cold wind.

'Whisper is getting cold Ryan. Come back,' Jack said now thinking if Ryan at least trained to be a dog handler for the time being what harm could it do?

'All right Ryan, but just to train for now. Do you understand?' agreed his forlorn sister.

Ryan reluctantly stood up to leave. 'I'll come back to the house then,' said Ryan as he held on Whisper's collar to pull himself up.

*

Three months later

Jack had placed the brown envelope on the side table in his sitting room. He was finding it hard to muster up the courage to open it. He knew it to be about Baz, but with him not returning with the rest of the battalion and, although presumed still alive but missing in action, he was terrified that this was proof he wasn't coming back. He paced the floor. Relieved when he finally managed to tear open the envelope and find it wasn't bad news after all. Baz had been found, injured but alive in a French hospital in Amiens and soon to return to England in the next couple of weeks. Jack couldn't wait to let Ryan and Vivien know.

In the last two months Ryan and Whisper had been training together at the Shoeburyness training school. This time Whisper was going to take a role as a scout dog. He was trained well as a messenger dog but the soldiers in charge needed more canines on the battlefield at all times helping with the casualties. Ryan would patrol in front of him on the terrain ahead and Whisper would detect every scent up to a thousand yards away. Whisper was being taught to raise his hackles and point his tail downwards, indicating that the enemy was approaching. It was too dangerous to bark. No more barking for Whisper now. Ryan could only think this was a good idea, but he hadn't let Vivien or Jack know. He knew how dangerous this was as frontline made them easy targets but it was a risk worth taking for the two of them as sometimes the dogs would carry medical supplies and these were vital. Ryan wasn't afraid of anything now. His stepfather had gone. He had been notified that he would be going to France with Whisper in a couple of months now, probably late January if they were ready.

*

January 18th 1917 - Battle of Ancre Valley, France

Christmas had come and gone and the celebrations at the White Lion tavern were as jolly as they could be due to the circumstances of the war. Some Australian and New Zealand soldiers who were training at a nearby barracks had joined the locals on Christmas Day, making the day especially entertaining with some playing Australian tunes on the piano, singing and teaching the locals typical Australian folksongs. Most of the young men from Three Shells Beach hadn't returned from France yet so at least these young Anzacs blew in a breath of fresh air for everybody.

It had begun to snow yesterday and Ryan was due to leave for France with Whisper. Concerns over Baz's well-being was very much on their minds. Instead of returning to England he had decided to stay on in France over Christmas but in his last letter to Vivien he had mentioned that he was feeling unwell again due to an aggravated leg injury and now, in hindsight, he felt he had made the wrong decision to not return home. That had worried them all and now not hearing from him again for a while, Ryan was keen to see what he could do and retrace Baz's steps out in France. Vivien was appalled at this and had begged him not to go but Ryan was adamant and nothing was going to stop him and Whisper in their mission to help Baz and others in trouble out in France on the Western Front.

Returning with the Essex battalion, Ryan and Whisper travelled to Ancre, near Miramont-de-Guyenne where they set up camp. Ryan knew his first duty was to rescue soldiers from the frontline but he also wanted to find out where Baz was and wondered whether he had returned to the frontline or was still recovering in hospital. The next morning their mission was to advance to Arles and capture it if possible with other regiments. But word was out that there were many casualties. Snow had blanketed much of the region and it was hindering the rescue of the soldiers. All the scout dogs and mercy dogs were on full alert with their soldier masters. Ryan would have to put off finding Baz for now and keep to his mission with the battalion. They set off at dawn and it wasn't long before they came across some soldiers from the Manchester regiment who were warning them to keep low as there was quite a lot of aerial fire further up the ridge. Before long, they reached a clearing beyond a wooded area and came across two aeroplanes that had been shot down. Ryan and Whisper stealthily made their way to the biplanes, aware that there was still fire being aimed at them from above. Whisper was close to Ryan's feet as they kept low to approach the smoldering aeroplanes. He could see a pilot in the front with another man behind him.

'Whisper, down!' Ryan instructed. Whisper started to bark loudly. Ryan became annoyed that Whisper wasn't doing as he was trained to do but as soon as Ryan tried to open the aeroplanes door, aerial fire came from the left, missing Ryan by inches. A soldier from the Manchester regiment fired back and killed the German soldier who was determined to hit Ryan. Another German soldier charged at them from the nearby wooded area, taking them by surprise. Just as he was about to aim his weapon at Ryan, Whisper lunged at him, knocking the German soldier backwards and leaving him unconscious on the cold icy terrain. Relieved to be still alive, and now crouching under the aeroplane with Whisper, Ryan instructed his scout dog to stay where he was as he tentatively stood up to thank the Mancunian soldier.

'Let's get these pilots out. We're all sitting ducks here,' he stated to Ryan, aware this young man was a novice and not experienced enough to know what to do.

Ryan and the soldier dragged the first pilot out to the

clearing with Ryan counting the minutes quietly to himself. Whisper now silent, but his tail down between his legs and whimpering slightly. Another dog, a mercy dog, was sitting by an aeroplane further on but the pilot was still and quiet and it was too late to save him. Ryan started to pull the German soldier, who he believed might still be alive back to the copse as the Manchester soldier pulled his pilot back to the copse as well.

'He is alive isn't he?' asked Ryan, looking at the pilot's head wound, his face covered in blood.

Whisper was licking the injured pilot's hand and Ryan was surprised at how attentive Whisper was with him, until he realised he was as familiar with the soldier as Whisper was. Ryan took out a rag from his pack and cleaned his face. Once he had cleaned the face of the now stirring pilot, Ryan couldn't believe who he was looking at. It was Baz!

'Let's get out of here,' declared the Mancunian as reinforcements came in with stretchers from the Essex battalion.

Piling the injured Baz onto the stretcher, Whisper yet again licked his limp hand that rested beside him. Walking beside Baz, Whisper looked up to Ryan for reassurance.

'Save me Whisper,' uttered Baz, before closing his eyes again.

'Good boy Whisper,' Ryan said, leaning down to hug him. 'You rescued us today alright my boy!'

CHAPTER 10 – THREE SHELLS BEACH 1918-1919

Bringing Baz back home to safety had been a major triumph for Ryan and Whisper. Whisper had had a write up in a local paper and Ryan was happy to be home and have Whisper safe and sound too. Baz's legs were broken and after a two month stay at a military hospital in Gravesend, he was sent back to the Coggeshall barracks. Vivien had visited Baz everyday that she had off from work. Baz had fallen in love with Vivien as she read to him, keeping him occupied from the boredom that had set in from not being able to walk. He was looking forward to being outside as the summer skies beckoned him back to Three Shells Beach.

As autumn became apparent with the early evenings drawing in, she asked Baz, while she sat by his hospital bed, 'Why don't you stay and recuperate at our cottage? You can spend the last few weeks of warm weather by Three Shells Beach. I can take a holiday from work and look after you. You are not fit for duty yet and with me looking after you, you will get on your feet quicker!' she suggested.

Summer had ended at Three Shells Beach and after weeks of picnics, Baz made a decision about his future. Now it was late November and the war had come to a close. The kite had been seen most days, sitting at the end of the jetty as if to keep a watchful eye on the couple. Baz was feeling stronger and no longer heard the cries of his fellow comrades in his dreams. The desolate land was a distant memory and the scenes of his aeroplane crashing in his mind's eye made him realise how lucky he was to be saved by Whisper and Ryan. Sitting on the beach, he compared the warm sand with the sticky mud he had been coping with out in France. Now he was safe here with Vivien, watching Whisper bounding in and out of the sea, making them laugh.

The next morning, Whisper woke Baz up by jumping on the bed and licking his face. Laughing and trying to push the dog off the bed, he heard Vivien's voice calling out to him saying she was going to work. He heard the door slam downstairs and tentatively got out of bed to watch her from the window. Her grey shawl around her shoulders made her seem tired and her body bent forward as she staggered along the beach in the now rousing wind. Her form touched him. She deserved better, he thought, and so did that boy Ryan who had become a man now. Their future was uncertain and he wanted to take care of that. He dressed quickly and taking a pen and some paper from the downstairs bureau, he began to write a letter to his uncle in Ottawa, Canada:

28th November 1918

Dear George

Thank you for your recent correspondence. I will take up your offer on the farm in Ottawa. Money will be sent soon. I have to finalise details here and then I should be on my way back to Canada early next year. I will be bringing my family with me.

Yours Sincerely

Your Nephew

Baz

Placing the letter in an envelope, he called to Whisper who was asleep under the kitchen table. 'Come on Whisper. We need to see Vivien at the post office and post my letter.

Let's hope for good news!' he said to the dog as he put on his collar.

Their injuries now repaired, they both ran up from the beach and along the coastal road together. Turning left onto the road up to the village, they ran straight passed Jack who was returning with his breakfast. 'Morning to you Baz! Morning Whisper. You both look well. A breezy day!' he said, eating a bite of his pastie.

'Thanks Jack. I'm going to ask Vivien to marry me,' he shouted back, leaving the old man on the edge of the beach with a broad smile on his face.

*

January 1919

The kite was seen once more. As the train left for Dover, Ryan sat nearest the window, picking at the padded upholstery nervously. Looking up to the darkening skies, he saw the bird. The kite was sitting once more on some railings, eyeing the train suspiciously. Ryan had a tear to his eye. He was saying goodbye to Essex, his home, the oyster fishing community, Three Shells Beach and his childhood. Jack Leemer was too upset to come to the station. They had said their goodbyes yesterday. Instead he stood on the jetty, looking out to sea, sad but happy for them. At least Ryan had Whisper at his feet to comfort him. Ryan could see there was something in the bird's mouth. An oyster perhaps, he thought. He wondered where the bird would drop the shell after it had eaten the tasty mollusc. Would it be in the sea, Three Shells Beach, or even the fields of France? He was curious of where his little family were going. Canada seemed so far away. A farm, he was told, where they would start a dog training centre just like the one in Shoeburyness. 'You would like that boy, wouldn't you?' Ryan asked Whisper as he had nuzzled the dog's neck, reminiscing about the time he had found out the good news that they were all to be a family.

Whisper licked Ryan's hand, comforting him, sensing that the train was ready to depart. The kite flapped its wings and soared into the sky as the trains whistle sounded, and an old man's life was going back to normal. For Ryan and Whisper, it was a new beginning.

THE END

The Soldiers Lament

To leave loved ones to fight another fight,

To soar like a bird, to carry on its work,

a shell that's left on No Man's land.

To watch where the people go across mountains and plains,

To watch the War unfold as it comes to a natural end.

ABOUT THE AUTHOR

Sophie Cloud's particular interests lies in military history and the dynamics of family life. Sophie loves the meaning of people's names and places. After she discovered that the first dog training centre was in Shoeburyness near to where she grew up, and for her love of dogs, she wrote her 'Coming of Age' novel 'Whisper'.

As a teenager, Sophie owned a Springer Spaniel called Sam who became a sniffer dog in the British Army after her family moved to London. Sophie wrote 'Whisper' whilst her dog Patches, a King Charles Spaniel, lay at her feet. 'Whisper' was written in memory of her dog Sam.

Sophie resides in London with her family.

Printed in Great Britain
by Amazon

57899027R00061